Lollipops

My Magic
Anorak

and other rhymes for
young children

Original Poems by **John Foster**

Illustrated by **John Wallace**

OXFORD
UNIVERSITY PRESS

Oxford University Press, Great Clarendon Street, Oxford OX2 6DP

Oxford New York

Athens Auckland Bangkok Bogotá Buenos Aires Calcutta
Cape Town Chennai Dar es Salaam Delhi Florence Hong Kong Istanbul
Karachi Kuala Lumpur Madrid Melbourne Mexico City Mumbai
Nairobi Paris São Paulo Singapore Taipei Tokyo Toronto Warsaw

and associated companies in
Berlin Ibadan

Oxford is a trade mark of Oxford University Press

First published 1999

British Library Cataloguing in Publication Data
Data available

ISBN 0 19 276208 7

Printed in Hong Kong

Contents

My magic anorak

I've got a magic anorak.
When I pull up the zip
It lifts me high up in the sky
Off on a magic trip.

I've circled round the Eiffel Tower.
I've been to Disneyland.
I've seen the Queen, who waved to me
And shook me by the hand.

I've had tea with Superman.
I've ridden in Batman's car.
I've had a picnic up in space,
Sitting on a star.

When I zip up my anorak,
I close my eyes and then
I count to three and off I go
On a magic trip again.

Bedbug, bedbug

Bedbug, bedbug, where have you been?
I've been up to London to visit the queen.

Bedbug, bedbug, what did you do?
I bit the queen's bottom!
I bit the king's too!

My old blue shirt

My old blue shirt
Is tattered and torn.
The collar is crumpled.
The elbows are worn.

The sleeve got ripped
When I climbed the tree.
There's a big dark stain
Where I spilled my tea.

But I don't care.
I like my old shirt
Though it's battered and tattered
And covered in dirt.

There's a hippo in the swimming pool

There's a hippo in the swimming pool
Splashing and thrashing about,
Whenever he gets near them,
The children scream and shout.

There's a hippo in the swimming pool.
He's like a wave machine.
He plunges down and then pops up.
He's like a submarine.

There's a hippo in the swimming pool.
He's driving us all mad,
'Cause the hippo in the swimming pool
Is Jason Johnson's dad!

Tony Maloney's skinny and bony

Tony Maloney's skinny and bony
Spencer Sprout is stout.
Grace Mace has a freckly face.
Sid Kidd's ears stick out.

And Peter Peck is a pain in the neck!

Geraldine Green's as stringy as a bean.
Bob Robb's big and strong.
Bessie Breeze has knobbly knees.
Liz Lee's legs are long.

And Peter Peck is a pain in the neck!

Mary Tipperary's very hairy.
Prue McGrew is small.
Percy Pratt is short and fat.
Tracy Tonks is tall.

And Peter Peck is a pain in the neck!

Shake your leg

Shake your leg, spin around,
Tap, tap your feet on the ground.

Waggle your bottom, wriggle like a snake,
Bend your knees and shake, shake, shake.

Flap your elbows like a hen,
Once, twice, again and again.

Clap your hands, clap, clap.
Click your fingers, snap, snap, snap.

Wave your arms up in the air,
Wave them here, wave them there.

Shake your hips, spin like a top,
Dance, dance until you drop.

At my ballet class

At my ballet class I learn
How to stand and how to turn;

To be a pretty flower that grows;
How to stretch and point my toes;

How to hold my head up high
And point my fingers to the sky.

Then my teacher shows me how
To bend my waist and take a bow.

My brother

Sometimes my brother sits
In his racing car.
In his helmet and his goggles,
He's a Grand Prix star!

Sometimes my brother wears
A big cowboy hat,
And gallops down the garden
Rounding up the cat.

Sometimes my brother wears
A mask and a cape
And chases all his friends
As they try to escape.

Sometimes my brother sits
And gazes at the stars.
He's travelling through space
On a mission to Mars.

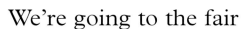

We're going to the fair

What will we do at the fair tonight?
What will we do at the fair?

We'll ride round and round on the roundabout.
Round, round, round.
We'll whirl and spin on the Big Wheel
High above the ground.

We'll swing to and fro on the swinging boats.
Swing, swing, swing.
We'll hook the ducks and win a prize—
A monkey on a string.

We'll ride in the dark on the ghost train.
Scream! Scream! Scream!
We'll buy a stick of candyfloss
And a huge ice-cream.

That's what we'll do at the fair tonight.
That's what we'll do at the fair.

Where are you going, Johnny?

Where are you going, Johnny-Just-For-A-Lark?
I'm going to play football down at the park.

Where are you going, Johnny-Head-In-The-Air?
To ride on the merry-go-round at the fair.

Where are you going, Johnny-Rushing-From-School?
I'm going for a swim in the swimming pool.

Where are you going, Johnny-Licking-Your-Lips?
I'm off to the fish shop to buy fish and chips.

Where are you going, Johnny-Looking-So-Glum?
I'm going into town to go shopping with Mum.

Dad's cooking pancakes

Dad's cooking pancakes for our tea—
One for you, one for you, and one for me.

Stir the batter in the bowl—
Mix. Mix. Mix.
Stir up all the flour and eggs.
Whisk. Whisk. Whisk.

Fry the batter in the pan.
Fry. Fry. Fry.
Toss the pancake in the air.
High. High. High.

Put the pancake on your plate,
Crisp and golden brown.
Sprinkle it with sugar
And gobble it down!

I like sizzling sausages

I like sizzling sausages.
I like bubbling beans.
I like cauliflower cheese
And different kinds of greens.

I like hot tomato soup.
I like chicken wings.
I like crisp fish fingers.
I like spaghetti rings.

I like eggs and bacon,
And Mum's potato cakes.
But most of all I really like
The fresh bread my gran bakes.

A week at Gran's

On Monday we went to the seaside
And I had a donkey-ride.

On Tuesday it rained all day.
We sat and played games inside.

On Wednesday we went to a fair
And I won a doll on a string.

On Thursday we went to the shops
Gran bought me this pretty ring.

On Friday we packed a picnic
And flew Grandad's kite in the park.

On Saturday we had a barbecue
And stayed up till it got dark.

On Sunday we packed our cases,
And Dad came in the afternoon.

As we waved goodbye, I shouted,
'Please can we come back soon!'

Footprints on the beach

Along the sandy beach, the footprints show
Who comes along and where they go.

Pawprints show where the young dogs bound,
Sniffing seaweed, chasing around.

Hoofprints mark the donkeys' tracks,
Where children ride upon their backs.

Boot marks show where fishermen stand,
Digging for worms in the squelchy sand.

Clawprints show where the seagulls tread,
Searching for scraps of picnic bread.

Bare foot marks show where children dash
Down to the sea to paddle and splash.

Along the sandy beach, the footprints show
Who comes along and where they go.

Weather Bear

Weather Bear,
Weather Bear,
Looks at the weather
Then decides what to wear.

It's hot today.
My T-shirt and shorts
Will keep me cool.
Then I'll put on my trunks
And jump in the pool.

It's raining today.
I'll wear my wellies
And my waterproof mac.
My umbrella will keep
The rain off my back.

It's cold today.
I'll put on a sweater
And a warm winter coat,
Thick gloves on my paws
And a scarf round my throat.

Weather Bear,
Weather Bear,
Looks at the weather
Then decides what to wear.

There's a snowman in the freezer

There's a snowman in the freezer.
He's wedged in very tight.
He says he's staying even if
It starts to freeze tonight.

There's a snowman in the freezer.
He's been in there all day.
He says he's hiding from the sun.
He won't come out to play.

There's a snowman in the freezer.
He says he'll only go
If we hire a plane to take him
Where there's a lot of snow.

There's a snowman in the freezer.
Hiding from the weather.
If we don't do what he wants,
He might be there for ever.

One for the spider

One for the spider and the web it's spun.
Two for the lizards basking in the sun.
Three for the rabbits scampering round.
Four for the hedgehogs snuffling the ground.
Five for the squirrels with bushy tails.
Six for the tracks of the creeping snails.
Seven for the ducklings paddling by.
Eight for the swallows swooping in the sky.
Nine for the kittens that leap and play.
Ten for the fieldmice hiding in the hay.

The mouse in the attic

There's a mouse in the attic
Hiding from the cat.
He's made himself a nest
In Mum's old floppy hat.

He wants to be a pop star.
He's written a new song.
He plays it on a banjo
And sings it all night long.

I went to the farm

I went to the farm and what did I see?
A cow that mooed and blinked at me.

I went to the farm and what did I see?
A pig that snorted and grunted at me.

I went to the farm and what did I see?
A sheep that baaed and stared at me.

I went to the farm and what did I see?
A hen that clucked and pecked at me.

I went to the farm and what did I see?
The farmer who smiled and waved to me.

I went to the farm and what did I see?
The farmer's wife who gave to me
A jug of milk and an egg for my tea.

Harvest time

Harvest time! Harvest time!
It's harvest time again.
Time to cut the corn
And gather in the grain.

Harvest time! Harvest time!
Time to pick the fruits,
To gather in the nuts
And dig up all the roots.

Harvest time! Harvest time!
In the autumn sun
We'll cut, pick, and dig
Until the harvest's done.

Autumn leaves

Autumn leaves are blowing
all over town,
covering the streets
in carpets of brown.

As fast as they rake them up,
more float down.
Autumn leaves are scattered
all over town.

On a starry night

On a starry night
The stars twinkle
Like thousands of bright eyes
Watching us and winking.

On a cloudy night
The stars are hidden
As if someone
Has blindfolded them.

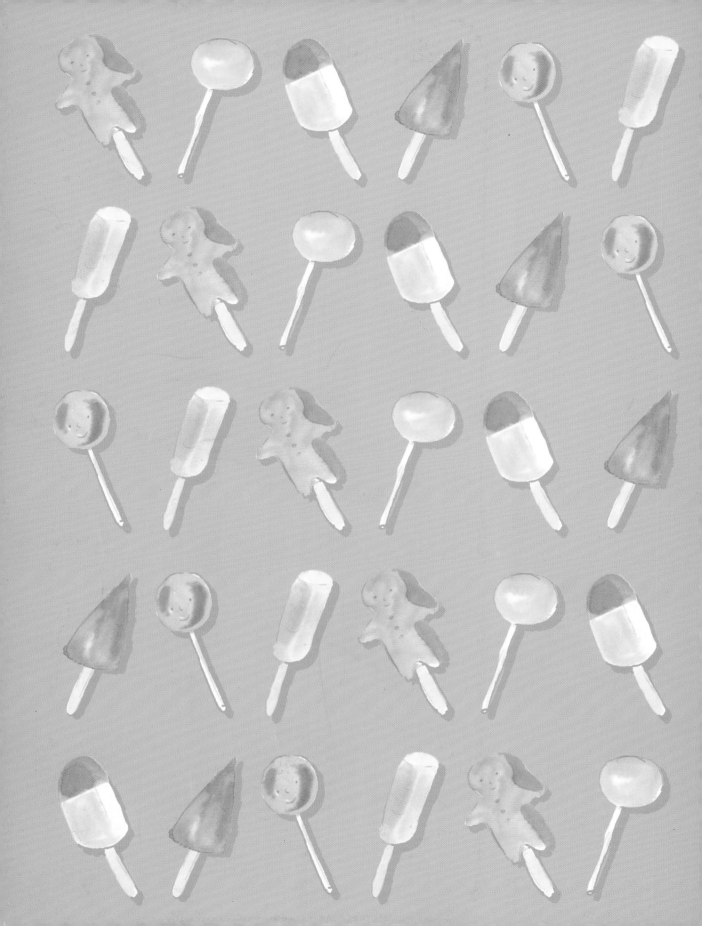